For Winston, my best bear

A FEIWEL AND FRIENDS BOOK
An imprint of Macmillan Publishing Group, LLC
120 Broadway, New York, NY 10271 • mackids.com

Our books may be purchased in bulk for promotional, educational, or business use. Please contact your
local bookseller or the Macmillan Corporate and Premium Sales Department at (800) 221-7945 ext. 5442
or by email at MacmillanSpecialMarkets@macmillan.com.

Library of Congress Cataloging-in-Publication Data is available

First edition, 2024
Book design by Naomi Silverio
This artwork was created in Procreate.
Feiwel and Friends logo designed by Filomena Tuosto
Printed in China by RR Donnelley Asia Printing Solutions Ltd., Dongguan City, Guangdong Province

ISBN 978-1-250-88305-6 (hardcover)
1 3 5 7 9 10 8 6 4 2

DON'T WASH WINSTON

WITHDRAWN

Ashley Belote

Feiwel and Friends · New York

Whenever Liam felt afraid, he turned to his best bear, Winston.

They could always
lean on each other.

The pair's favorite game to play was pie factory.

But one Saturday, while Liam was preparing a fresh batch of pie filling . . .

Filling

CAUTION CAUTION CAUTION CAUTION CAUTION

Winston took a terrible tumble.

Liam watched as his bear flipped toes over nose with a . . .

Squish

Squo

Winston needed washing.

"I can't go in there with you, Winston . . .
We won't be together! And what if you don't
come back?!"

"Plus! The washing machine is loud."

"It's big . . ."

"And you'll be locked in a box full of water! I don't think so."

Winston was NOT getting washed.

"Just remember . . .
Don't. Look. Down."

But it wasn't long before his hiding place was discovered.

SQUAWWWK!

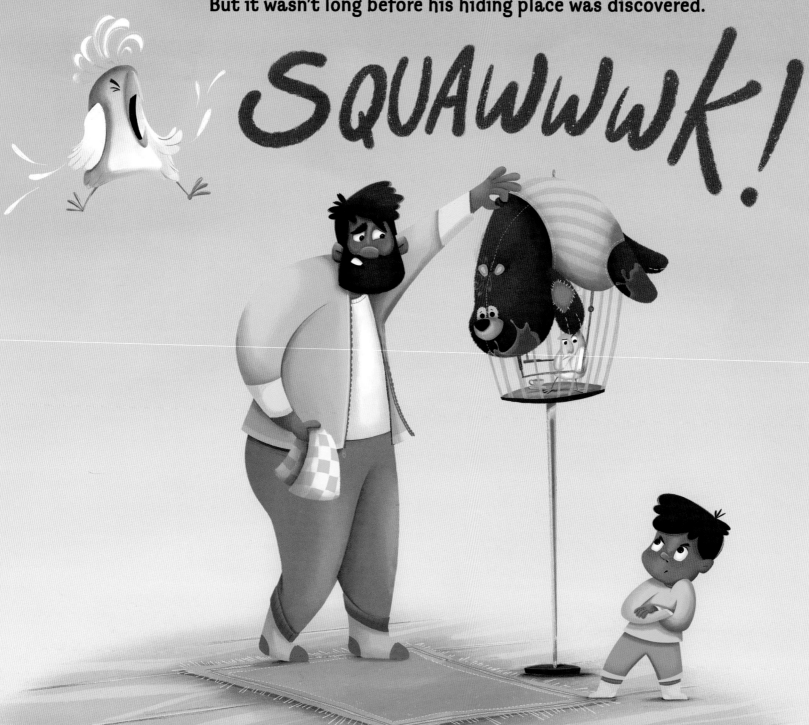

"I have a better idea, Winston."

"You'll be safe in here."

But he wasn't.

WOOF! WOOF! WOOF!

"I have a new plan."

"One final piece to top it off . . . plus a snack."

"Almost done . . ."

"Ta-da!"
Liam had created the perfect disguise.

"It's pie time, Win— I mean, Bar-bear-ian!"
As they were returning to their stand . . .

Liam slipped, then tripped,

then toppled over . . .

right into the puddle
of filling!

"Oh no!"

Liam needed washing.

He hopped in the tub and scrubbed up all clean. "That feels much better."

Then he looked over at Winston . . .

Liam realized what
had to be done.

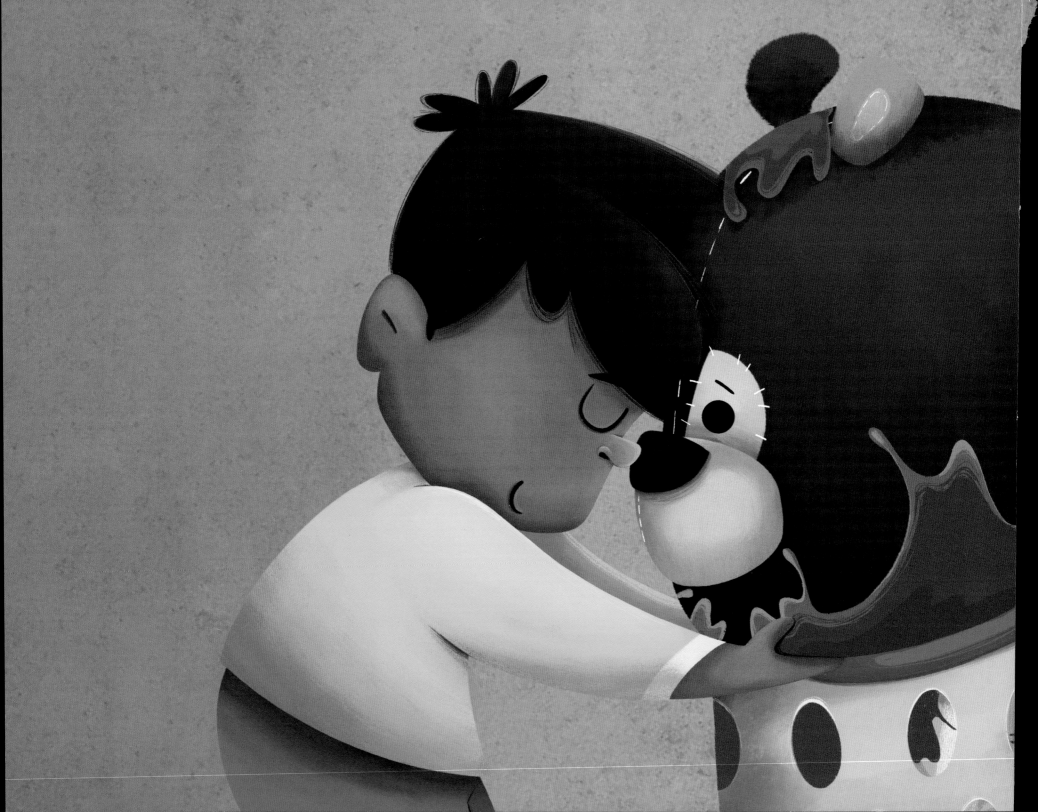

It was time to face this fear and do what was best for his best bear. Winston really needed washing.

"I'll be right here waiting the whole time," said Liam.

Winston was
finally . . .

washed.

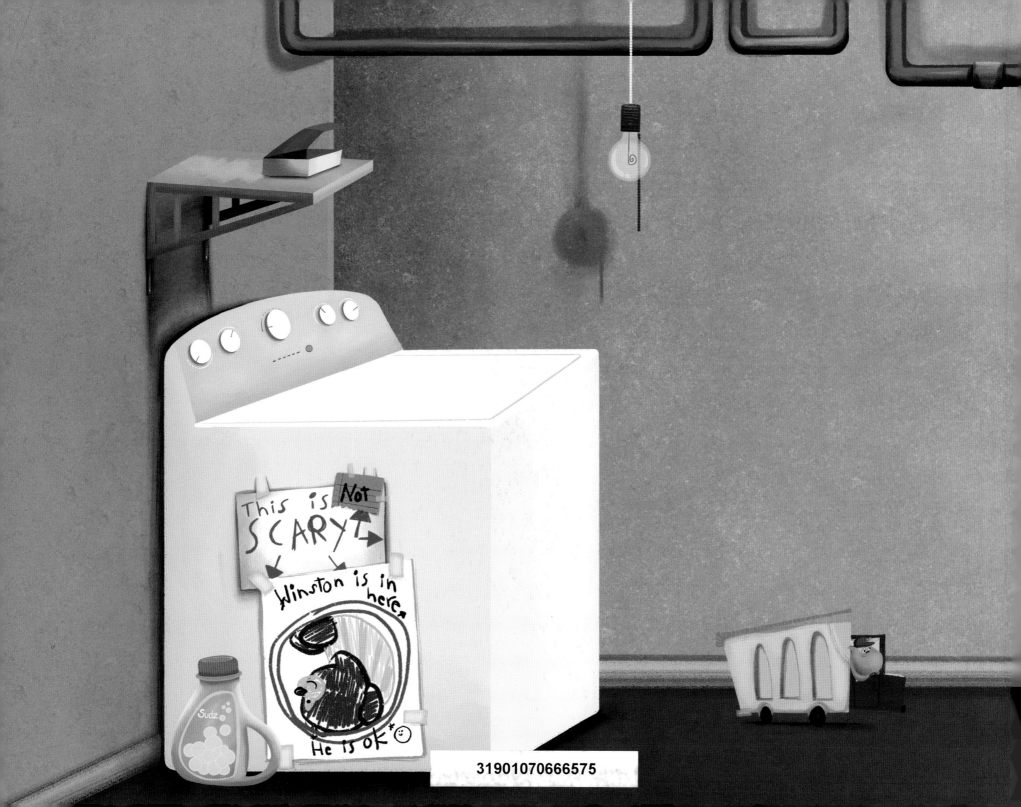